This book brings you
glad tidings for Christmas
and a happy New Year

T O

Ben + Jackie 2010

F R O M

Love - Granny xx

We Wish You a Merry Christmas

ILLUSTRATED BY

Michael Hague

Henry Holt and Company

NEW YORK

We wish you a merry Christmas,

we wish you a merry Christmas,

we wish you a merry Christmas

and a happy New Year!

Glad tidings we bring

to you and your kin,

*Glad tidings for Christmas
and a happy New Year!*

Please bring us some figgy pudding,

Please bring us some figgy pudding,

*P*lease bring us some figgy pudding,

and bring it right now!

We won't go until we get some,

We won't go until we get some,

We won't go until we get some,

so bring it right now!

*W*e wish you a merry Christmas,

we wish you a merry Christmas,

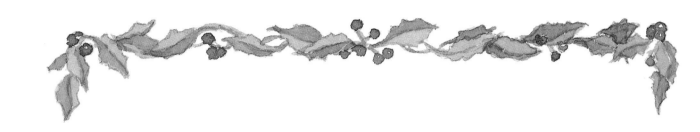

we wish you a

Merry Christmas

and a

Happy New Year!

Library of Congress Cataloging-in-Publication Data

Hague, Michael.

We wish you a Merry Christmas / illustrated by Michael Hague.

Summary: An illustrated edition of the traditional Christmas carol.

ISBN 0-8050-1629-5 (LARGE-FORMAT EDITION)

1. Carols, English—Juvenile literature. 2. Christmas music—Juvenile literature.

3. Folk-songs, English—Juvenile literature.

[1. Carols, English. 2. Christmas music. 3. Folk songs, English.] I. Title.

PZ8.3.H11935We 1990

782.42'1723—dc20   90-32067

Special Edition | Designed by Marc Cheshire

Printed in the United States of America on acid-free paper